Reagandoodle & Little Buddy
WELCOME BABY

Sandi Swiridoff with Wendy Dunham
Illustrated by Michal Sparks

HARVEST
Kids

HARVEST HOUSE PUBLISHERS
EUGENE, OREGON

The Scripture quotation at the end of the book is taken from the Holy Bible, New Living Translation, copyright © 1996, 2004, 2015 by Tyndale House Foundation. Used by permission of Tyndale House Publishers, Inc., Carol Stream, Illinois 60188. All rights reserved.

Cover design by Mary Eakin

Interior design by Left Coast Design

Published in association with the William K. Jensen Literary Agency, 119 Bampton Court, Eugene, Oregon 97404.

HARVEST KIDS is a trademark of The Hawkins Children's LLC. Harvest House Publishers, Inc., is the exclusive licensee of the trademark HARVEST KIDS.

A portion of the proceeds from the sale this book will help support foster-care families.

Reagandoodle and Little Buddy Welcome Baby

Copyright © 2019 by Sandi Swiridoff and Wendy Dunham
Artwork © 2019 by Michal Sparks
Published by Harvest House Publishers
Eugene, Oregon 97408
www.harvesthousepublishers.com

ISBN 978-0-7369-7466-0 (hardcover)

Library of Congress Cataloging-in-Publication Data
Names: Swiridoff, Sandi, author. | Dunham, Wendy, author. | Sparks, Michal, illustrator.
Title: Reagandoodle and little buddy welcome baby / Sandi Swiridoff with Wendy Dunham ; illustrations by Michal Sparks.
Description: Eugene, Oregon : Harvest House Publishers, [2019] | Audience: Age 4-8.
Identifiers: LCCN 2018023012 (print) | LCCN 2018024188 (ebook) | ISBN 9780736974653 (ebook) |
      ISBN 9780736974660 (hardcover : alk. paper)
Subjects: LCSH: Labradoodle—Anecdotes—Juvenile literature. | Human-animal relationships—Juvenile literature. | Adoption—Anecdotes—Juvenile literature. | Foster home care—Anecdotes—Juvenile literature.
Classification: LCC SF429.L29 (ebook) | LCC SF429.L29 S97 2019 (print) | DDC 636.72/8—dc23
LC record available at https://lccn.loc.gov/2018023012

Printed in China

18 19 20 21 22 23 24 25 26 27 / LP / 10 9 8 7 6 5 4 3 2 1

LITTLE BUDDY

REAGANDOODLE

My name is Reagandoodle, but most people call me Reagan.

This is Little Buddy, my best friend. He's two and a half years old.

Since I'm older (in dog years), I'll be the one telling this story about the newest member of our family.

The very first day Little Buddy and I met Baby Girl, the sky turned bluer.

The sun shined brighter. Even the flowers grew just a little bit taller.

That's because the whole world smiles when a baby comes home.

When Little Buddy and I met Baby Girl, she was only two days old.

She was wrapped in a tiny pink blanket, all snuggly-bug warm, with just her face peeking through.

Little Buddy and I looked at her. We waited for her to do something.

But Baby Girl did nothing.

She didn't open her eyes. She didn't talk. She didn't smile.

She simply stayed wrapped up in her tiny pink blanket,
all snuggly-bug warm.

Since Baby Girl didn't do anything, I decided to sniff her.

She smelled clean and sweet and fresh—not at all like my dog bones.

When I sniffed Baby Girl, she smiled.

Little Buddy thought that was funny, so he sniffed her too.

When Little Buddy sniffed Baby Girl, she smiled even more.

We were so excited, Little Buddy laughed and I barked.

We were very loud. This made Baby Girl cry.

Little Buddy and I quickly learned that Baby Girl does not like loud noises. But…

...Baby Girl does like kisses.

Since we want to make Baby Girl happy, we give her lots of them.

We kiss her cheeks.
We kiss her fingers.
We kiss her elbows.
We kiss her nose.

We even kiss her ten piggy-toes.

Baby Girl does not like her diaper changed.
She wiggles all over and doesn't hold still.

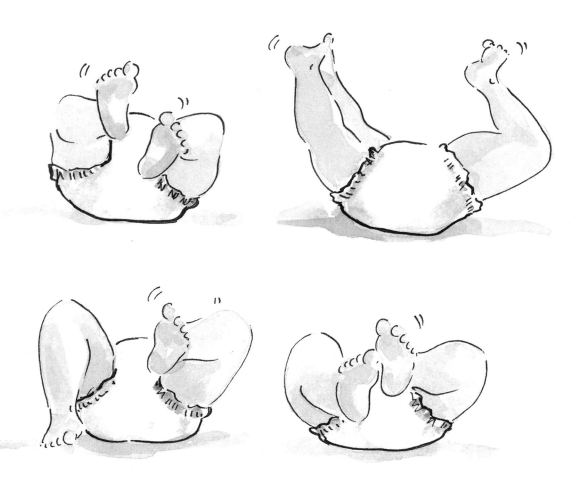

This makes it difficult. But Little Buddy and I help
every way we can.

Baby Girl smiles
when Little Buddy and I tickle
her tummy. Since we want to make
Baby Girl happy, we tickle her tummy
whenever it's bare.

Little Buddy loves tickling. Being a good tickler is an important job for a big brother.

Baby Girl does not like to be cold. When she's cold, Little Buddy and I help by bringing her tiny pink blanket to Mama.

Mama knows how to swaddle Baby Girl so she is happy and warm.

Baby Girl is glad when Little Buddy and I help feed her.

Since we want to make Baby Girl happy, Little Buddy
and I help however we can.

Little Buddy and I have also learned what Baby Girl can't do. Baby Girl can't talk like Little Buddy or bark like me.

But she can make funny noises. This makes Little
Buddy laugh.

Baby Girl can't ride bikes, like
Little Buddy and me. And she can't run or
fetch, like Little Buddy and me. But one day, she will.

Right now, Baby Girl is best at snuggling.

Baby Girl likes to hear Little Buddy and me sing. Since we want to make Baby Girl happy, we sing "Jesus Loves Me" before she goes to bed.

Little Buddy loves singing. Singing is an important job for a big brother.

Baby Girl is especially good at sleeping. She sleeps all day. She sleeps all night. When Baby Girl is sleeping, Little Buddy and I play quietly.

We read books. We play with puzzles. And we draw
pictures. We are good helpers by playing quietly.

Since Baby Girl joined our family, many things are different.

Little Buddy and I were used to only the two of us.
I had Little Buddy to love, and Little Buddy had me.

But now that Baby Girl is here, Little Buddy and I have one more person to love, and one more person who will love us back…

...and we wouldn't trade that for anything!

Here are photos of the real Reagandoodle, Little Buddy, and Baby Girl. Reagandoodle is a special kind of dog called an Australian Labradoodle. When he was eight weeks old, he was adopted by Little Buddy's grandparents.

Little Buddy became a foster child when he was eleven months old. He was later adopted by his foster parents. Now he has a forever family.

Baby Girl has joined their family as a foster child.

Dear beautiful child,

God builds families in many different ways. Sometimes a baby grows inside a mama's tummy, and when the baby is born, they stay with the same mama forever.

Sometimes a baby grows inside a mama's tummy, but then after the baby is born, they are adopted, and God sends a new mama who will love them just as much and for as long as forever.

And sometimes babies and children join foster families. They might be with those families for only a little while. But some of those babies are adopted by the foster families and stay in that family forever.

No matter what kind of family you have, and no matter how you've joined your family, you can be sure that God especially chose you and your family to be together. He did that because he loves you.

You are incredibly special!

With love and hugs (and a whole bunch of licks!),

Reagan and Little Buddy

God places the lonely in families
...and gives them joy.
Psalm 68:6

Sandi Swiridoff is the "momager" of @Reagandoodle on Instagram. She and her husband, Eric, have two grown children and one famous fur-son (Reagan, of course). They are also very proud grandparents (one of their grandchildren being Little Buddy!). Besides spending time with her family, Sandi's greatest joy is using her gift of photography to bring smiles and encouragement to others while benefiting children in foster care.

Wendy Dunham is an award-winning inspirational children's and middle grade author, a registered therapist for children with special needs, and a blessed mama of two amazing grown-up kids. She is the author of two middle-grade novels: *My Name Is River* and its sequel, *Hope Girl*. She has a series of early readers titled Tales of Buttercup Grove. And in *Reagandoodle and Little Buddy Welcome Baby*, Wendy writes as the voice of Reagandoodle. Please visit her website at wendydunhamauthor.com.

Michal Sparks' artwork can be found throughout the home-furnishings industry in textiles, gift items, dinnerware, and more. She is the artist for *Words of Comfort for Times of Loss*, *When Someone You Love Has Cancer*, and *A Simple Gift of Comfort*, as well as the Tales of Buttercup Grove series of children's books. Connect with Michal at www.michalsparks.com.